D

New Year

C.M. Serpell

About the Author

C.M. Serpell lives in the South West of England with a growing collection of four legged companions.

She spent most of her career working in a prison. Whilst there, she worked with men convicted of a wide range of offences. She worked in various roles from rehabilitation and substance misuse, to teaching business start-up and social enterprise. She has now hung up her keys and fulfilled a lifelong dream of becoming a published author.

This is a work of fiction. Names, characters, places, and incidents either are the product of the author's imagination or are used fictitiously. Any resemblance to actual persons, living or dead, events, or locales is entirely coincidental.

First paperback edition October 2024
ISBN 978-1-7393659-8-1 (paperback)

Contact:
www.cmserpellauthor.co.uk
Instagram: @cmserpellauthor
Facebook: C.M. Serpell Author

Dedication

Eddie and Arthur.

Author Note

Short stories. Something a bit different.

I loved writing Her, Him, and Until Death, but I wanted to try something different. Don't worry, a full-length novel is in the pipeline for next year.

Short stories have been a minefield. It seems to me that the rules are… there are no rules! Some people like long, some short, some twists, some leave on a cliff hanger. For this reason, you can only rely on two things with this collection of short stories – they all have death and winter themes. Some are darker, and some have a slightly more comedic edge. I would love to know which ones you enjoyed most. Perhaps you will see some of these characters again one day…

Contents

Spider

If I told you it's about a cabin in the woods, the possibilities would be endless. So, I'll just say it's about a cabin in the woods!

Troy

My eyes adjusted to the gloom as I began to take in my surroundings. The room was dry, the temperature pleasant. Stamping my foot, the hollow sound told me there was a wooden floor beneath the loose dirt. Despite it being winter, it was a still day with nothing to hear, not out there in the woods anyway.

As the thought that no one was around struck me, my skin tingled. Did that mean no one would hear a scream? I'm not sure where that thought came from, but I'm sure I didn't imagine the temperature dropping. I rubbed the goosebumps on my arms.

I'd played in those woods all my life but never found the hut before. I was intrigued, but there was another feeling. I couldn't put my finger on it, but I remember rubbing my arms, trying to warm my skin to make the goosebumps disappear. I had a sudden overwhelming urge to get away.

My bike was where I left it, on the leaves outside. The bright red frame contrasted with the mud and rotting leaves on the forest floor. Whilst I wanted to get away, I also wanted to make sure I could find the camouflaged hut again. Picking up my bike, I noticed a tweed lead hanging from the handlebars. It reminded me how I ended up there. Looking around, there was still no sign of my dog.

Kit

The cold damp fabric surrounding my body woke me early. I squeezed my eyes closed as the familiar salty smell told me why my bed was wet. I knew Mum would be mad. She said I should have grown out of it by now. The crack in the curtains suggested it was too early to get up, but I couldn't just lay there waiting for my punishment. As I peeled my wrinkled pyjamas from my body, I shivered. It was another hour before the heating came on. I screwed the offending garments into a ball and stuffed them down the side of the bed before hunting around for my school uniform. I planned to go to my special place. I hadn't been for a few days.

My bike was on the path where I left it, despite mum nagging me to put it in the shed. I quietly wheeled it away from the house and got on when I was on the road. I would go to my special place. The darkness made everything louder; the breaking of twigs and sticks as I cycled onto the woodland footpath echoed around me like mini gunshots, and the leaves rustled as if they were whispering to me. I was never frightened in the woods, though. Even with only the moon to guide me, I easily found my cabin. I hesitated at the door. Something was different today. At the time, I wasn't sure if I imagined it, but I was sure the door wasn't how I left it. My heart raced as I pushed it open in anticipation of what I would find.

As my eyes adjusted to the gloom, I saw the cabin was empty. I rummaged in my school bag for my torch and balanced it on a ledge in the grooved wall. The room filled with shadows, and enough light for me to find the loose floorboard. Sinking to the floor, I leaned down and pulled out a large wooden tray. The tray held several pots containing my projects.

I held each pot up, one by one, inspecting its contents. I had more work to do, but I wanted to wait until daylight; until I could do it properly. Carefully putting them back into the hole, I replaced the floorboard and scuffed some loose dirt over the top. I felt calmer. The shed was my happy place. The work I did there gave me a sense of control. I would come back after school.

Troy

I woke early, filled with anticipation like Christmas morning. I couldn't wait to go back to the shed. Something pulled at me like a magnetic force. At the time, I didn't know what it was. Looking back, I still don't know. It was a feeling I can't explain. Perhaps it was a sense of danger: I sensed something about the shed was important.

I was tempted to head there before school but didn't think I would find it in the dark. I don't often take my bike to school, but that day, I rode so I could go straight to the woods after. As soon as I could, I hurried from the school gates, careful not to attract attention, and cycled towards the woodland. There weren't many people around at this time of year – school would break up for Christmas a few days later, and the cold made people go straight home in the evenings. Checking over my shoulder, I joined the muddy path, trying to retrace my steps - looking for familiar trees or clearings. I saw the hut, camouflaged by greenery and looked around before wheeling my bike towards it. There were fresh tyre marks outside the door. I looked around but couldn't see another bike. There was no sound coming from inside. The feeling of danger shivered down my spine. I say danger. Maybe it was excitement.

I crept towards the door and slowly pushed it open. There was someone crouched on the floor. The boy was from a different school; I recognised his uniform, but without seeing his face, couldn't tell if I had seen him around. He didn't move when I came in. He was so intently focused on what he was doing. I stayed silent and risked a side step, trying to get a better look at what had his attention.

Kit

I returned to the shed after school. All day, I was excited to get back and continue with my project. I kept the spider in a pot for a few days and had begun removing its legs to see how long it would survive. This was the day I was to remove leg number three. I wasn't sure what to feed spiders, but I left a few squashed flies in the container with it – I didn't want it to die of starvation before I could finish my experiment. I held a pair of tweezers in each hand; one to hold the spider still and the other to remove a leg. The leg came free, and I shook the tweezers to drop it on the floor - that was when I noticed him watching me. Preparing for him to tell me off, I hastily shoved the lid on and jumped to my feet. It was then that I looked at his face. He wasn't angry. I recognised the emotions on his face, the smile spreading across his cheeks. It was as if I was looking into a mirror.

Before I could say anything, he asked if I was going to pull another leg off. A spark caught my eye as he flicked the lighter in his hand.

The spider didn't make it to the Christmas holidays, but I knew in that moment, I had a new lab partner.

The Housewife

Is revenge always sweet?

Then

Her eyes followed the red stain as it spread in the snow, the harsh contrast as beautiful and alarming as the wintery assault on the landscape. The figure before her didn't move; there was enough blood that she could tell there was little hope. 'Revenge is sweet,' she hissed as she bent over the figure in the yellow coat.

Now

Jane blinked and looked at the ground before her. The unblemished snow was pure and virginal, settling in soft gentle waves where the fine powder coated the landscape. A snow-covered wreath lay in the spot where a figure in a yellow coat once fell. A tear rolled down Jane's cheek, and she gasped, trying to get air into her lungs as her breath caught in her throat. The iron vice surrounded her body, an unrelenting claw gripping onto her. Her raspy breathing caused her to panic. This was not the first time the iron vice had taken hold. As she looked around, the world span and moved faster than her eyes; houses and snow blurring together. Focusing on one house, the familiar house, she remembered what her therapist said. *Concentrate on your breathing, slowly breathe in through your nose and out through your mouth.* As she remembered the gentle voice, she regained control of her body. The house was the same, but different. It had been painted the same colour, but was fresher than when she last saw it. The smoke billowing into the sky told her its residents had the fire lit. She closed her eyes and inhaled, searching her senses for the warmth of woodsmoke. She was back in the house, the fire lit and hot chocolate bubbling on the hob. Their home was picture-perfect; filled with laughter, baking, cosy blankets on the porch swing. They were happy. She knew every loose floorboard, every groove or knock in the fabric of the house. It was her home.

It had been fifteen years since she was last here, but the pain wasn't any less real. Prison was never going to be easy for someone like Jane; a housewife, a school mum. She was used to baking for school fairs and keeping a timetable of after school clubs and sports kits. She wasn't used to the rash that cheap clothes gave her, or eating mass produced prison food cooked without love. Nights had been the hardest – alone with her mind. The cell itself was quiet, but the building never slept – Jane hadn't known which was louder, the other residents, or the screaming inside her head. The pain was so intense, she felt it, heard it, swirling around her, dragging her down into the thin mattress, the springs of the bed below digging into her slight frame.

The other prisoners shunned her. She learned fast to keep her head down and not try to spark any friendships. She was among the lowest of the low. Most crimes were accepted, but not hers. The other women looked at her with disgust; some went as far as to spit at her. They all knew who she was; her case made national news.

The prison sentence had been lonely, but Jane knew release would be even lonelier. Her parents didn't speak to her after that night. Her now ex-husband deserted her. Her friends deserted her. After all, who would want to be associated with her after what she did?

Standing in the cold, fresh snow swirling around her, Jane looked across the street at the house she used to share with him. The house they lived in after Jane was forced to move out. She couldn't understand why she'd to leave when he was the one who'd had the affair. '*She isn't stable enough to look after her daughter,*' they said, '*She isn't thinking straight.*' She couldn't understand how she had ended up in prison. Of course she wasn't thinking straight, her whole world fell apart when her husband invited another woman into bed with him.

Dropping to her knees and brushing the snow from the wreath, Jane let out a moan. *It wasn't supposed to happen.* She gasped as the holly pricked her finger leaving a smear of red in the snow. The stain spread before her eyes, and she was back there again.

That night.

The yellow coat.

It belonged to her husband's new wife.

She always wore it…

Then

Jane watched the house from under the trees, her hand wrapped tightly around the smooth handle of the knife in her pocket. The lights were on, and she imagined them playing happy families, but it was her family. Her happy family. She gripped the knife tighter, her knuckles turning white in her pocket, and squeezed her eyes shut. When she opened them, her 'replacement' was at their car across the street. The car door slammed, and as she turned in the direction of the house, Jane sprang towards her, quickly closing the gap between them. She raised the knife, then brought it down in one swift movement. It struck the side of the hood, piercing the thin material, along with the jugular of its wearer. She took another aim, keeping hold of the blade as the second blow caused the body to fall to the floor. The steel glinted in the moonlight, a red glow where blood streaked across the blade. She bent down, her heart racing, threatening to burst from her chest, hissing the words, 'Revenge is sweet,' as she bent over the figure in the yellow coat, pulling back the hood. She stumbled backwards as the hair revealed was blonde, not the brunette shade of her husband's new wife. Dropping forward onto her knees, she clawed her way back to the body, her breath caught in her throat. As she moved the hair away from its owner's face, her daughter's glassy eyes stared back at her.

Solid Ground

Some people are just impossible to please.

Marge sighed as the shovel reverberated when it hit the solid ground. The winter had been mild, but the fresh snow had rendered the land undiggable within a few short days. She scanned the landscape for inspiration, interrupted by a car door slamming. Throwing the shovel to the ground, she carefully climbed the snow-covered slope leading from the edge of the woods up toward the fence that would take her back to the edge of the guest area.

Alongside her own cottage, the small holding housed three wooden lodges which she ran as a successful holiday lettings business. Climbing the styal, she spotted the gleaming car, specked with dirt from the country lanes. A woman stood beside it, taking photos of the scenery. She looked up as she heard Marge approaching, and dropped her phone in the leather handbag hanging from her elbow.

'You must be Faye.' Marge held her hand out.

'Hi. Great to meet you. The place is lovely.' Faye took Marge's hand.

'Let's get inside where its warmer, and I can show you around and then I'll let you get settled.' Marge led Faye toward one of the lodges. The rustic exterior carried through to the inside of the property, complimented with large fluffy throws, giant sofas and a log fire crackling.

'I love it already!' Faye exclaimed, her eyes shining as she looked around the room. 'I just needed to get away for a few days, and this is the perfect hideaway!'

Marge showed Faye where everything was and offered to return before night fall to see if she needed anything, pointing in the direction of her cottage should she need anything in the meantime.

'Are there other guests here?'

'Just you and a couple in one of the other lodges. We had a gentleman in the third lodge, but he checked out earlier than expected. So, I'm not expecting anyone else.'

'How lovely. The reviews online are amazing, so I can't wait to get settled and take a walk before trying some of your home cooking that everyone raves.'

Marge smiled. 'Yes, people are so kind leaving those wonderful reviews. I really am blessed that my guests are so thoughtful.' Their conversation was interrupted by a man's voice shouting Marge's name. 'I must go, it sounds like one of the other guests needs me. Marge's smile dropped as she turned away from Faye and headed in the direction of the voice that was cutting through the snowy silence outside. He was standing beside Faye's car, looking around as Marge approached. She fixed the smile back on her face as she asked him what was up, leaving off the word now.

'This car is right in the way of our view. How long's it going to be here? Also, the fire has gone out again.'

Assuring him that Fayes car was only there while she unloaded her luggage, Marge stepped past him to look at the fire. The man's wife opened the door to the cabin, wrapped in blankets.

'My wife is freezing. Look at the state of her.'

Marge moved to the log burner. Smoke inside the burner made it impossible to see through the glass door. As she opened it, smoke leapt out into the room, causing the man to cough in a theatrical fashion. The logs hissed. Maggie grabbed the poker and prodded them. 'I take it you ran out of logs and decided to put wet ones on the fire?' She didn't wait for an answer before continuing. 'As I said when you arrived, and as it says on the log basket, please let me know if you need more logs, and I can bring you a basket. I advise all guests not to gather their own firewood. Wet logs won't burn.'

'We couldn't find you.' The man answered back.

Maggie fixed the smile back on her face before turning to face him. 'I have been here all day, either in my cottage or making up the lodges either side of you. I'm sorry you are cold, but this is why the guidebook is there.'

'I don't need a guidebook to keep a fire going.'

Choosing to ignore his comment, Maggie let him know she would bring more logs and get the fire sorted before dinner. The couple had created problem after problem since their arrival a few days before.

Returning to the cottage with logs, she was pleased to see Faye's car had been moved already. She tapped on the couple's door, holding up the bag of logs. 'Do you need me to get the fire going again?' The man snatched the logs, declaring he was capable of doing it himself. She took the opportunity to remind them of the dinner menu and said she would be preparing it to bring and serve in two hours.

'Perhaps you could avoid putting salt on the dessert this evening.' The man's wife spoke without looking up from the magazine she was reading.

Maggie had already explained to the woman that morning that salted caramel dessert had salt in it, and that was the menu choice selected on arrival. Each guest was given a menu to select their meals for the duration of their stay. The woman had found something not to her liking with every meal so far. Maggie rarely had trouble with guests, but between these and the man who was in the third lodge, the week had been tiresome. She could just tell these were the sort of people that would leave a bad review. She prided herself on the star rating her business held on TripAdvisor. The reviews praised her cooking, her hosting skills, and showed that people noticed the personal touches she applied to every stay. She made sure guests wanted for nothing. The ungrateful guests were few and far between; it was just typical that she had two dodgy bookings so close together and right after the snow fall.

Double-checking the menu, Maggie was pleased to see all three guests had requested the same soup as the starter for their meal. She delivered each course to the guests freshly cooked in her kitchen at allocated meal times. She pulled ingredients from cupboards and shelves to prepare the pumpkin spiced starter. The meat was in the slow cooker, simmering away. Taking her granite pestle and mortar, Maggie set about grinding up the extra ingredients for the couple's soup. The radio played Christmas songs, cheering her mood somewhat. As she poured their soup into a thermos to take to them, she sprinkled in some of the crushed sleeping pills and holly berries. Whistling as she crossed the garden to deliver their starter, she couldn't help but smile at her quick solution. They glared at her as she set it in the small kitchen area for them. The unorthodox way of serving meals allowed guests to eat in private without having to prepare their own meals.

By the time she arrived with dessert, the couple had already passed out in the lounge. The curtains were drawn, so she put another log on the fire and pulled the door closed so she could return after dark. Glancing at the styal marked 'no entry, unsafe terrain', she considered the previous guest abandoned, wrapped in tarpaulin beside her discarded shovel. He was also hard to please. He threatened to leave her a bad review, and that would never do.

The Black Dog

A story about loss.
(Don't worry, the dog doesn't die!)

That bloody dog, again. It's been hanging around ever since November this year. I remember because there were still Halloween decorations around, and I thought to myself, it won't be long before Mariah Carey is playing on every radio station and the city centre will be filled with Christmas parties. I'll make an excuse not to go to ours, the same as every year.

Anyway, the dog. It was just there when I looked out of the window one morning. I saw it skulking around on the green opposite our house. I say, our house, it's just me here since, well, it's just me here. I feel for the poor thing out there; it's skin and bones. Since that first sighting in November, I've been feeding it. Amy would have been cross with me, but she's not here now. She was never a bad person, wouldn't wish ill of the dog, but she would say we shouldn't encourage it. We had a cat once. He was six when he got run over. We swore we would never get another pet

- the pain of the loss was too hard to bear. I know some may say he was only a cat, but he was our cat. Amy couldn't have children, so Gizmo was our baby.

We agreed we were happy without children. We tried. We tried so many times. And then we agreed not to try. We agreed Gizmo was our baby. Then our baby died. Amy said it brought back the trauma of loss all those years before. The early pregnancies that she just couldn't carry, the pregnancies that ended with a flush. It took so much to even get that far - the injections and all the appointments, only for it to end with the inevitable heartbreak.

We grieved for our unborn babies, and we grieved for Gizmo. Every time we experienced another loss, we lost a bit more of ourselves. But we always had each other. I knew that whatever life threw at me, Amy would always be at home waiting for me.

One day, out of the blue, Amy decided enough was enough. She was here one minute, and the next, a pair of police officers were standing in our living room.

I saw them coming up the path, hats under their arms. I knew something was really wrong when they took their hats off. It wasn't long after that the dog started visiting me. The snarling old thing recognised a sucker like me, perfect for a visit from the black dog.

She wouldn't have felt a thing, they said. Death would have been instantaneous, they said. My world tilted on its axis. That aways seemed a strange expression, I thought, until it happened to me. Life really did tilt on its axis. It was me and her against the world. Whatever happened, we always had each other. Until we didn't. Until I was left alone, just me and the black dog.

I've thought about campaigning over the years. Trying to raise awareness, especially at this time of year. Is it hypocritical to think of doing that? I know I probably never will, but I see posters and campaigns and think that perhaps I could do something. Make a difference.

Sadly, we see it too often around Christmas, they said. The driver was drunk, they said, and failed to stop at the crossing. She wouldn't have felt a thing, they said again.

Enough is enough, she said. We can't go on hiding from the world in this bubble of grief. It's not good for us. I was drunk. I promised I would stop drinking, cut down, whatever it took. Reminded her, we were better together, stronger. The tears ran down her cheeks, and it took all my self-control to stop myself going to her. And then. Then she walked out of my life for good. I followed her; of course I did. She was fast. I went back for the car. I knew I shouldn't be driving. I'd had far too much to drink.

I sped along the roads, looking for her. How did she disappear so quickly? I took the road into town. I know I took the corner too fast. I couldn't stop. I tried to stop. It was too late. I didn't even see what I hit. It was all a blur.

I kept driving.

I came home, put the car in the garage and poured myself a drink to steady my nerves. I promised myself I would stop, whatever it took to make her stay. But in that moment, one more wouldn't hurt. I finished my drink and checked the garage was locked. The car was dented. I looked away, turned off the light and went in search of another drink.

It wasn't long before the police car pulled up outside. The driver didn't stop, they said. No one saw it happen.

I didn't know it was her. I didn't know. I should have stopped. Why didn't I stop? The shock was genuine, the grief real.

My world tilted on its axis that day, the day I killed my wife.

Her Last Photo

They say a picture tells a thousand words.

Sarah pulled the car between the old stone pillars, eying the tatty signs, warning the site was patrolled by security. Clouds hovered over the old factory, casting shadows in the already bleak landscape; rain hung in the air, threatening to fall. Sarah avoided broken glass and kept driving past various buildings until she could turn the corner and park out of sight of the road.

Driving past the factory each day, Sarah was intrigued by its desolation. Today, she finished work early enough to visit and explore. She loved looking at websites and Facebook pages featuring abandoned places – attracted to the eeriness of buildings no longer habited. With a good eye for photography, she had curated an attractive selection of images for her social media. With four or five buildings to choose from, Sarah was confident she would get some good pictures. She held her phone up snapping some exterior shots while the rain held off. The first building was securely closed up. Graffiti caricatures on the wooden boarding laughed at her futile attempts to gain entry.

Glass crunched underfoot as Sarah approached another building. This time, there was nothing stopping her from entering. The room opened into an old factory floor with offices on a mezzanine level, presumably to look out over the workers. More shattered glass lay around the windows. Stepping further into the building, she stopped and listened. There were no pigeons or birds, the quiet road wouldn't see many visitors, and there were no other apparent visitors to the site.

Sarah was completely alone.

She looked back at the doorway, car keys in hand, then pulled her jacket around her and stepped further into the concrete abyss. Archways led to darkened rooms and corridors with faded signage advising which areas were restricted. As she approached one of the side rooms, a different scene greeted her. The windowless room looked like it had been inhabited at some point, more recently than the factory itself. She hesitated again, looking back at the door to the building before returning her gaze to the room. Peering into the darkness, she saw the ventilation shaft from the ceiling hanging precariously, surrounded by dangling cables. Waste and what looked like personal belongings were strewn around. There was a pile of scorched paperback books. The remains of what looked like a bonfire were in the middle of the room. Kicking the books, she smirked as she noted a copy of one of the 50 shades of grey books.

A noise caused her to spin around, butterflies flapping furiously in her stomach as she mentally prepared an excuse for why she was trespassing. There was no one there. The cavernous space looked the same as when she entered. Taking a few deep breaths, she turned back to the room and held her phone up to take some photos. The gloomy light as the sun began to set added to the creepy aesthetic.

She froze. That noise again.

Taking her keys from her bag, she calculated how long it would take to run to the car if needed. There was no sign of anyone between her and her car. Her heart rate quickened; her skin tingled.

Did I imagine it?

She stepped out and gulped in the fresh air. Her breathing slowed, and she told herself not to be so silly. Looking up at the sky, the clouds appeared to be twisting and turning, getting darker as they moved. She didn't have long to explore. The winter nights drew in quickly at this time of year. The silence was deafening, as Sarah's breathing slowly returned to normal. Moving back into the building, Sarah surveyed the concrete steps. She tentatively took the first couple of steps, braced for any movement. They held firm, and she proceeded up the staircase. The old offices were strewn with paperwork, filing cabinet drawers hung open, and office chairs had the stuffing hanging out of them. From her vantage point, she could see the factory line below.

Sarah knew from Googling the factory that it had shut down 36 years ago when the company went bust. From here, she could imagine workers busy at their stations, chatting and bustling about their days. An arrow graffitied on the wall caught her eye and she moved down the steps heading for the corridor. More graffiti said, *this way*. She followed the trail, ignoring the goosebumps prickling her skin. As she moved through the factory, she noted the doors to the rooms were closed. Peering through the porthole style window of one of them, her reflection stared back at her in the darkness. Progressing into the building, the light stayed behind. The rooms were windowless here; natural light limited. Something underfoot caused her to pause. She looked down at a red stain on the floor, surrounding her shoe.

It's probably just tomato sauce, someone's idea of a prank.

She pulled her phone from her pocket, cursing as the slowness of her dated model caused a lull before the torch came on. More shadows appeared in the darkness, a dark red handprint smeared on the wall ahead.

She froze.

It's just sauce, it's just sauce.

Sarah shook her head, putting aside thoughts of horror films.

People don't get murdered in abandoned buildings in real life.

Sarah's heartrate thundered in the quiet corridor. Nervously smiling, she turned the torch off so she could take a selfie with the 'bloody' handprint. As she looked down, switching her phone back to the torch, a shadow loomed before her. Before Sarah had a chance to scream, a large pair of hands gripped her throat. Her phone fell to the floor as she clawed at the fingers around her neck. Sarah's legs turned to jelly as everything went black.

The smiling image was her last photo.

The Family

Relatives can be stressful.

Fiona sighed. The stand-off had reached its eighth minute, and her youngest child decided he would not be forced to stay in his highchair until his plate was clear. Elliot launched a tree of broccoli from his position, quickly followed by more trees and his cutlery. At 18 months, he knew what he wanted, and right now, he was focused on getting out of eating his vegetables.

Fiona sighed, again.

Elliot screamed.

Fiona squeezed her eyes shut.

Hermione approached her brother. 'Shhhh,' she soothed, 'Father Christmas won't visit if we are naughty.' Her little brother's face lit up as Hermione spoke to him; the crying stopped, and he focused his wide blue eyes on her face. Elliot still didn't eat the remaining food.

The front door slammed, and Fiona, Elliot, and Hermione paused, looking expectantly at the kitchen door. 'I'm home,' came the cheery greeting. Taking in Elliot's red face and the food debris littering the kitchen, Tom scooped Elliot from his high chair. 'Did mean Mummy try to make you eat those nasty vegetables again? Don't worry, Daddy's home now.' Elliot's blonde curls bounced as he giggled at his father's words. Tom put him down on the floor and moved to kiss his wife on the cheek. 'Right, I'm off for a shower. I said I'd meet the lads for a couple of pints. You don't mind, do you?' Tom left the room before Fiona could respond.

Free from the confines of his high chair, Elliot was just about to pull a bag of flour from the open cupboard when Fiona intervened. She looked longingly at the front door.

'Mummy?' Hermione's voice interrupted her thoughts. 'Yes, darling?'

'Can we watch a film?'

'I need to get your brother in the bath, but you can, yes.'

The steam smacked Fiona in the face as she opened the bathroom door. Pushing through it, she moved to open the window and put the bath running. Elliot toddled in the direction of her bedroom and she called out for Tom to keep an eye on him while she picked up Tom's discarded work clothes and wet towel which lay beside the laundry basket.

'Can you take him?' Tom handed Elliot to Fiona.

'I'm just trying to tidy up while the bath runs.'

'I'm not being funny, Love, but you have all day to do that stuff. It would be nice to come home to a tidy house once in a while.'

Wordlessly, Fiona took Elliot from her husband and turned to the bathroom. She soon heard the stairs creak as her husband descended. A vision passed before her eyes - her husband, lying at the bottom of the stairs in a crumpled heap, his lifeless eyes staring at the ceiling. She suppressed a giggle as she massaged the shampoo into her son's hair.

With squeaky clean hair and skin, Elliot was wrapped in a towel, ready to dress in his pyjamas. As she moved to pull a pyjama top over his head, Fiona breathed in the familiar scent of her son. His blue eyes, her husband's eyes, locked on hers. 'Mummy, story?'

'Of course, darling, which one shall we read?'

'No!' Elliot's lower lip jutted out. 'Daddy read.'

'I'm afraid Daddy's out tonight. He will be back later and can read you a story tomorrow. Elliot's face reddened, and Fiona pursed her lips while she waited for the screaming to start.

Four hours later. Elliot continued to scream. Hermione sat in the corner of the room, crying silently. Fiona sat beside her daughter; her eyes squeezed shut.

The door slammed, and all three of them went quiet. Tom dropped his keys in the bowl and the stairs creaked as he ascended until he peered into the room.

'What's happening? Why is everyone in Elliot's room?'

Hermione spoke pointedly. 'You promised to read him a bedtime story before you went to work this morning.'

'You promised to help me wrap the Christmas presents this evening before your parents arrive tomorrow.' Fiona whispered.

Elliot sniffed.

Tom held his hands up. 'I thought you had things under control, and it would be okay to meet my friends for a quick drink. I work hard you know, while you get to stay home with the kids. I deserve a bit of time for myself now and again.'

Fiona said nothing.

Hermione was the first to move. Her old soul declared, 'Now you're home, Daddy, and things are under control, I'm going to bed.' She moved to where her father crouched beside her brother's bed and wrapped her arms around him.

'Night darling.'

Hermione left the room, glancing at her mother, who remained on the floor, on the way out.

Fiona didn't notice. Her eyes were shut, and she massaged her temples.

'I thought you had everything under control. Is it too much to expect to be able to have a few Christmas drinks with friends and come home to find the house in order?!'

Fiona briefly made eye contact with her husband, opening her mouth to speak, then closing it again.

Her husband continued his tirade. 'I trust you have everything in order for Christmas? Don't forget Dad needs to watch his salt levels, so be careful you don't over season the food! Oh, and Mum said she hasn't had time to do the Christmas puddings. I told her not to worry and that you would sort it.'

'It's too late to get an online delivery now. I'll have to go to the shop tomorrow evening if you will be home on time?'

'Can't you go while I'm at work?'

'Elliot is going through a difficult phase, and I can't face the supermarket with him.'

'It's one toddler.' Tom laughed. 'How hard can it be? I know you never really wanted kids. Sometimes I can see why.' He laughed again.

'Dessert and not too much salt. Got it.' Fiona spoke through gritted teeth. 'I'll leave you to settle Elliot, if that's okay? It's you he wants.'

Tom's back was already turned as he sat on their son's bed, a book in hand.

As she got ready for bed, Fiona looked at the photos in their bedroom. A picture of her in her wedding dress, her late parents either side of her. Tom holding Fiona in his arms outside the door to their first house. Their sun-kissed faces smiled back at her from a beach in Fiji, where they went for their honeymoon. Her eyes moved across the photos, scanning their life as they grew older, as the children appeared. Her eyes darkened, and she quickly changed into her pyjamas before slipping under the cover and turning the bedside light off.

Fiona lay in bed, her eyes gently closed, her senses heightened as Tom moved around the bedroom using the light from the landing. The bed dipped as he got in and kissed the back of her neck before rolling to face the opposite wall. Fiona opened her eyes, remaining motionless, listening for the sound of her husband's rhythmic breathing.

She lay still as the minute hand on the clock moved around its orbit. It passed the number 12 three times, and still she lay. Her body didn't move, but her mind didn't stop.

The hand passed the 12 twice more before she gently rolled from the bed. She reached for her phone, then left it, glancing back at her sleeping husband.

Creeping from the room, Fiona took a bag from under the stairs and filled it with clothing from the airer, stopping briefly to change from her pyjamas.

Her passport was in the console table in the hall. She slipped it into her bag and took a look around.

More photos. Faces smiling at her.

Her wedding day. The day her best friend told her to always have a nest egg; a backup plan.

Her honeymoon. Tom told her he would always love her, and they didn't need children to be complete.

Her first baby scan. An accident. Fiona told Tom she still didn't want children.

She moved silently to the kitchen, checking that the back door was locked, the key safely in a drawer before she turned the gas oven on. Back in the lounge she lit a candle, closing her eyes for a brief moment, before leaving the house, careful to lock the door and drop the spare key in a flowerbed.

Fiona looked back at the dark house, the weight lifting, swirling above her like a dark cloud being taken away by the wind. She turned toward the woodland across the road from where she lived and let the moon guide her way along the footpath. She thought back to her childhood. She always knew she didn't like being around children. Even as a child, she avoided them. She told Tom she didn't want them, but he had to push it. She didn't want to lose him.

And now?

A loud bang echoed in the silent night.

Now she had lost him anyway.

Liquid Gold

What if there was something you could drink that would make everything okay?

Kitty looked across room through the glass wall into her Manager's office, and then back at her computer. The unread email gave no clue as to its topic, but Kitty immediately felt her stomach twisting into knots.

What could be so important that she had to send an email?

Her manager was on the phone, not looking in Kitty's direction. The other admin staff were busy at their desks. Kitty heard the tapping of nails on keyboards, telephone conversations, phones ringing, the ping of the elevator. She swallowed and returned her gaze to her desk, clicking to open the email.

'Dear Ms. Balm.
Re. Disciplinary Hearing.'

What?!

'You are invited to attend a formal disciplinary hearing on Monday 18th December at 2:30 pm.'

Two weeks away?

'The hearing is to discuss the following concerns:

1. Attendance and time keeping
2. Company policy regarding use of alcohol'

Fuck. Fuck, fuck, fuck, fuck, fuck.

The rest of the words blurred on the page as Kitty looked around the room again. No one was looking at her.

Do they all know?

She blinked, fighting the tears that threatened to spill over her eyelids. Her manager was still facing the other way. Kitty hastily scribbled a note saying she wasn't feeling well, was going home early, and could her colleague let their manager know when she was off the phone. She dropped it on the keyboard of her colleague, who was away from her desk, picked up her bag and hurried from the room, using all her energy to avoid breaking into a run. As she broke free from the building, she gulped in the fresh air before vomiting onto the pavement. An older woman wrinkled her nose and tutted loudly as she passed by.

Wiping her mouth, Kitty pulled a pack of mints from her bag and felt around for her aluminium water bottle.

Fuck.

She rummaged some more, and her heart sank as she realised she had left it on her desk. Stepping away from the vomit, she pulled her coat around her and headed for the newsagent. Christmas music filled the shop, and foil decorations hung from the ceiling. She bypassed the reduced advent calendars and individually wrapped Christmas cards and scurried to the till.

'Just a small bottle of vodka, please.' She asked the cashier.

'That'll be £8.95. Anything else?'

'No thanks.' Kitty moved from one foot to the other, trying not to snatch the bottle from the cashier as it was handed to her. She took it and put it in her bag, striding from the shop with the small bottle in her bag, holding her attention. It was a short walk down the street to her flat, but her eyes scanned the park opposite. She ran across the road and into the barren urban woodland. Bare trees lined the paths, and she walked quickly, until she was out of sight of the road, before finding a bench. Eyeing the wet wooden slats, she pulled the bottle from her bag and twisted the metal cap until the familiar click as the seal broke. Putting the bottle to her lips, she took a deep breath before pulling large gulps of the liquid into her mouth. She ignored the burning sensation as it ran down her throat. As the warm feeling spread through her veins, like liquid gold warming her body, she sank down onto the wet bench and sobbed.

She used to enjoy a glass of wine after work, it helped her to unwind, to relax. Kitty always had difficulty sleeping, even as a child, but when she had a drink before bed, it was much easier. It was just a glass to unwind and sometimes another to help her sleep. There were a couple of occasions when she had a glass of wine to settle her nerves at lunch time. She told herself plenty of people had a drink with their lunch. When she didn't sleep, Kitty was so tired in the mornings, but if she had a drink before bed, she was equally groggy. A couple of sips of wine from the bottle before she left the house would perk her up, and it's only a couple of sips, she reassured herself. The water from the bench seeped through her black work trousers, the cold seeping into her skin. Kitty thought back, trying to remember when she started filling her water bottle with vodka.

How do they know? No one knows. I get my work done. I don't make mistakes.

Kitty had been late a few times, but it wasn't her fault. She had to wait for the newsagent to open on a few occasions when she drank too much the night before and had nothing left to pick her up before work. She screwed the lid back onto the bottle and peeled herself from the seat, shaking her legs to unstick her soggy trousers from her wet skin. The bottle was nearly empty.

Ah well. In for a penny….

She drained the bottle, screwing the metal cap back on and dropping it into a bin as she crossed back through the park.

'Just a bottle of vodka, please. A large one.'

The cashier gave her a sympathetic smile.

'I dropped my bag and the last one smashed.' She smiled at the cashier, suddenly aware of the vodka on her breath and took a step back, stumbling.

'That's £14.99. Cash or card?'

Kitty fumbled in her bag, producing her debit card to tap the machine, this time snatching the bottle from the cashier.

'Kitty! Kitty! Is that you?'

She froze.

'How are you feeling? I got your message that you weren't feeling well. The boss wasn't happy, but you can't help being ill.' Kitty's colleague gave her a conspiratorial wink.

'I- I, er- I was just getting some medicine to settle my stomach, and I am going straight home to bed. Thanks for passing the message on.'

'You don't look too well. Do you want me to call you a taxi? Should you be walking home if you aren't well.'

'I'll be fine.' Kitty hastily retreated from the shop, scurrying across the road and back to the bench. She carefully sat in the dry spot and looked around her. It was getting dark already. Although surrounded by city, the park was quiet at this time of year, with people hurrying to get home in the warm. As the darkness grew, Kitty sipped from the glass bottle, letting the alcohol wrap around her body like a warm blanket. A rustle in the bushes caused Kitty to look around, giggling as she almost unbalanced on the bench. Righting herself, she peered into the darkness.

'Hello?' She slurred. 'S'no one there. It's just my imagination.' She reassured herself. 'Should probably go home anyway.' Willing her stiff legs to pull her to standing, they gave way, and she giggled as she landed back on the bench.

Discuss the company alcohol policy. Who do they think they are? It's them who have driven me to drink.

Kitty tried to stand again, blinking slowly as her head spun. She cleared her throat and shook her head, wobbling as she tried to clear her vision, before falling back onto the bench.

Maybe I will just lie here for a few moments.

Kitty closed her eyes as the alcohol pulled her under. The cold seeped around her body, reaching for her bones, pulling her body temperature down. The vodka kept her peaceful and unaware as hypothermia took hold.

The Autopsy

It started with a Y-incision.

Life is never without its ups and downs. Maybe we need the downs so we appreciate the ups more. The past month has been a real mixture for me. Forgive me. I don't want to get maudlin. My true intention is to tell you about my week. The week I finally get to fulfil one of my life goals.

I've worked in the funeral home for a few years now. It's something I have wanted to do since I was little and watched My Girl. Do you know that one? It's the one where McCauley Culkin's character dies from a bee-sting, and Jamie Lee-Curtis and Dan Ackroyd fall in love. If you haven't seen it, you must. Anyway, Jamie Lee-Curtis plays a makeup artist who ends up working in Dan Ackroyd's funeral home doing make up on the dead people. From a young age, I was fascinated. Fascinated with death. Fascinated with what happens to us after death. We don't all get Jamie Lee-Curtis doing our makeup, but we will have our own makeup artist. A dedicated person, or team of people who will see to our hair, do our makeup, and even paint our nails! I sometimes wonder if nail technicians get jealous of the mortuary assistants… after all, their clients are much easier to keep still. Anyway, this is where my story began.

Now of course, little girls are supposed to be cute, and I learned quickly that telling people you want to work with dead people when you are older doesn't go down well. I told my teachers and any other grownups who asked that I wanted to be a makeup artist. I neglected to mention that it seemed more interesting if my clients were dead.

Life swept me away, and the dream stayed in the back of my mind, like a box under the bed that I would get out to look at from time to time. I was swept along by school, by boyfriends, girlfriends, and life. Life wasn't always kind to me. School wasn't great. I have some good memories, but they are few and far between. For the most part, I existed as a verbal punch bag for the school bullies. As an adult, I made some poor choices and ended up with my beautiful baby girl, Rachel. From the moment she was born, she was the light of my life. I would do anything for her. Rachel was what some might call serendipitous - a happy accident. Did I intend to get pregnant from a one-night stand? No. Did I know the man I had sex with would turn out to be controlling, manipulative, and, at times, plain abusive? Also no. We tried to work as a couple a few times over the years. Each time I managed to end it, he would worm his way back in. He promised he would look after Rachel and me, that things would be different. He promised he wouldn't hurt me. He always did. Luckily, he never laid a hand on Rachel. Dear, sweet Rachel.

Where was I? Ah yes. So, I went to college and got all the certificates I could in makeup and beauty. I figured, how hard could it be to transfer the skills used on a living person to a dead one?

I saw the advert. The funeral home nearby was looking for mortuary assistants. I carefully completed an application form, being sure to note all of my certificates. I enclosed a cover letter explaining how much I wanted to work in the industry; and how I felt my skills were transferable. When they offered me an interview, I couldn't believe my luck. Finally, this was my time. I wanted a place to belong, and I knew that this was it. It took a while to find my feet. The others had worked there a long time - they knew each other, laughed and joked together. The funny thing with death is, well, it's not funny. That's the thing. Even though death isn't funny, to work with death, you have to find your own sense of humour. We are always respectful. We always care about the dead. But, without a sense of humour, it would all be so incredibly tragic.

When relatives drop off photos and clothes and explain how they want their loved ones to look is one of my favourite parts of the job. The body on the trolley suddenly comes alive. Not like that! What I mean is, they become a person again. Not just a corpse. The family often linger to tell us stories. I love to hear what the person did with their life, about their achievements and experiences; their family and loved ones. Older people are the best. They have often lived such rich lives, and I love to hear their story.

A few years in and I know this is the industry I want to work in forever. I want to learn it all. I want to know about embalming and post-mortems; especially post-mortems. It has always been a dream to watch one. A live one. Not just a video or one on the TV. I think I have the stomach for it – I don't pass out at the bodies doing my job, so it can't be much different.

Anyway, this week has been a bit different for me. I finally have the opportunity to watch a post-mortem! I can't believe my luck. I've spent more time at work in preparation. Rachel is staying with mum. I have been in every day and today is finally the day I get to watch it happen. The pathologist, we call him Mort, is the perfect person to watch. Usually, he shuts the door, and what goes on in the room is a mystery. Well, it isn't a mystery really, because I have watched many post-mortems online and read so much about them. But it feels mysterious when he shuts the door. I bet you are wondering why Mort is in the funeral home. It's a funny sort of set up. The pathologist wouldn't usually work from the same premises as the funeral home, but we are lucky the services are all in one building.

This morning, when I woke up my, head was all over the place. I could barely remember where I was. With Rachel at Mum's, it was so quiet on my own. I don't think I have ever had this much quiet. I love my family, but I can't say that I haven't enjoyed some me-time. I was so cosy, lying in the dark thinking about the day ahead. The day I get to watch a post-mortem. I want to remember every moment.

Mort prepared the room. The deal was that I could watch but wouldn't have an active part in the task at hand. I can't put my finger on what was wrong with Mort today. He seemed quieter than usual, a little despondent. It wasn't the time or place to ask what was wrong.

He got to work in an orderly way, and I loved watching him set out his tools. They gleamed in the lights, clean and sparkling in the sterile environment. He wore his usual plastic apron to cover his lab coat and quickly set to work making the first incision. Now, this is where I wasn't sure what would happen. If there was a moment I got queasy, I felt sure this was it. I paused and waited for the nausea that didn't come. After making the Y-Incision, Mort began to peel back layers of flesh and get to work. It was a methodical and calm thing to watch. He was so careful, making precise incisions and movements. The care with which he lifted out organs and gently placed them on the scales filled me with admiration for this gentle man. He worked through the organs piece by piece, logging the details on his chart. When the time came to put them back in the body, I noticed him pause and take a deep breath. He does this every day; I didn't expect him to be so affected. It's nice to see that he hasn't become blind to the importance and enormity of the task ahead of him.

He continued folding flesh back into position and carefully began stitching. The neat rows of stitches were a thing of perfection. Mort finished the procedure and tied off the thread, following protocol and putting equipment and waste into designated areas. He then zipped the bag closed and stood for a moment. His head was bowed, so I moved where I could see his face. I stayed out of his way until now. As I moved closer, I spotted the moisture glistening in his eyes. Reaching out, I put my hand on his. He looked down as our skin met, saying nothing before moving and pushing my body back into the refrigeration unit. I step inside to lie with my body. I don't feel cold. I feel snug and safe, zipped into my bag.

My body is at peace now.

Some people look for signs when they are around the dead. They want to know the person is still with them. They want to know death isn't final. As Mort went to turn off the light, he glanced around the room. His eyes fell on the trolley where I left him a single white feather.

I finally got to watch a post-mortem today.

Sisters

There is no better friend than a sister.

The world twirled and spun in a sea of colour and shapes; cold air whipped against her face, and she kept spinning and twirling until the flash of steel hurtled towards her. In that moment, the world stopped moving as a river of red swirled around her, clouding her vision until everything went black.

24 hours earlier

As the gravel crunched, Sam was alerted to the car on the driveway. 'Babe, go help my sister with her bags will you.'

'She's a big girl. I'm sure she can bring her own bags in. Maybe then she will learn to pack lighter.'

Sam threw a tea towel at her husband, her face telling him that the request wasn't optional.

She looked out of the window as her husband approached her sister's car. They both looked at the window and she held her hand up in greeting. Her sister and her husband had never been each other's biggest fans, but as the years went by, they found a comfortable rhythm.

Her mind drifted back to the conversation she had with her sister in the car on the way to her wedding. Her sister asked if she was sure Ben was the one, her tone implying she didn't think he was. Sam asked her sister why? What did she mean? What did she know? Her sister shrugged. 'Nothing,' she said, 'just a feeling. Ignore me, go get married!'. They had never mentioned it again, but it was always there, hanging over the marriage like a grey cloud on the horizon. Over the years, she had asked Ben why he disliked her sister. He always shrugged, saying it was in her head. Fast forward twelve years and two children, and she had learned to accept it.

A pair of arms wrapped around her waist as Sam shook her head, shaking the memories away. 'Hey, sis,' she said, leaning into the hug, breathing in the familiar scent.

'Auntie Jane, Auntie Jane!' Identical boys ran into the kitchen. 'What did you bring us?'

'What did I bring you? I brought you me! Aren't you lucky?!' She reached out, catching hold of one of the wriggling boys and tickling until he begged for mercy.

'I've put your bags in the guest annex. The heating is on in there, so everything should be all set for you.'

Jane straightened up as her brother spoke, releasing her nephew. Clearing her throat, she thanked him and made excuses to go and unpack. She stayed with her sister's family every Christmas and relished the opportunity to spend quality time with her twin nephews. Their vast property had a guest annex attached to the main house, large immaculate gardens, and a meadow. The meadow offered wildflowers and apple trees in the summer, whilst in the winter, the large shallow pond froze quickly, allowing them to skate on the lake. Sam raised her boys to be outdoors in all weathers, and Jane enjoyed that they weren't like most of her friend's children, propped in front of screens as much as they could convince their parents to allow.

Putting her suitcase in the large hall cupboard, Jane noticed the door to the main house was ajar. She pasted a big smile on her face, looking down expecting to see the boys had snuck in. Her face dropped as she took in the empty hallway, the tinkle of Christmas music drifting in from her sister's kitchen. Closing the gap between herself and the door, she closed it and pulled her top off, heading for the bathroom. Wiggling out of her travel joggers, she leaned into the shower cubicle to put the water running. She stiffened as she felt a hand on her back, resting on the elastic at the top of her knickers, its thumb gently rubbing her hip. Her heart raced as her body responded to her brother-in-law's touch. His hand moved around her back as she turned into him, tilting her head up for a kiss.

'I've missed you.' He muttered into her ear before gently tugging on her earlobe with his teeth.

'We can't.... I only just got here... Sam-'

'Shhh, she's busy in the kitchen. She won't even notice we are gone.'

'But, the boys-' Jane stopped speaking as her brother-in-law gently trailed kisses down her neck, stopping at her collarbone and moving back to her mouth. Looping her thumbs into her knickers, she let them drop to the floor and turned away, stepping into the shower, the water running over her invitingly. Ten minutes later, they emerged from the shower, hastily grabbing towels and drying their bodies before stepping back out into the hallway. Jane looked at her brother-in-law when she saw the connecting door was ajar. 'I definitely closed it.' She whispered.

'I'm sure you just didn't close it properly. I'll go first; I need to get logs from the shed anyway.'

Jane took a deep breath and waited until she heard the back door slam closed before following the Christmas music to the kitchen and asking her sister what she needed help with.

'Everything is all under control. Why don't you pour us both a glass of wine and then go see what the boys are up to.'

With the boys in bed, extra logs on the fire and a bottle of red wine open, Sam and Jane settled on the sofa. 'So, tell me, what's new with you? Is there a man on the scene?'

Jane laughed. 'You think I would be able to keep it to myself if I met someone?! You know you would be the first person I'd call.'

'There must be some news? No online dating tales to share with your old married sister?'

'No, really! I deleted all the dating apps. I just can't be bothered with them. Half the men on there are married anyway.'

Sam looked at her sister. 'Is that a problem?'

Jane stiffened.

'Maybe you are better suited to being a glamourous mistress? All the fun, with none of the boring responsibility.' Downing the last of her wine, Jane stood, declaring she needed a top up. Sam followed her to the kitchen. 'Seriously though, would you ever date a married man?

'What are you on about? Of course I wouldn't.' Jane's back was turned to Sam as she selected a bottle of wine from the rack. 'Do you have a preference, or is this one okay?' She said as she held up a bottle of Châteauneuf-du-Pape.

'Why don't we go have some fun instead?'

Jane looked at her sister's eyes, shining in the dimly lit kitchen. 'What are you thinking?'

'Let's go down to the pond!'

'I don't know if that's the best idea. We have both been drinking.'

'Well, we can stay here, and I can continue grilling you on your love life if you'd rather?'

Jane grimaced as she agreed.

Earlier snowfall left a thin coating on the grass that crunched underfoot as they made their way across the garden; the floodlights unnecessary under the watchful beam of a full moon. As the pond appeared before them, Jane hesitated. 'Are you sure it's frozen?'

'Of course. We have been skating on it for a few weeks already. Are you too chicken, little sister?'

Jane brushed the snow from the bench and sat to change into her skates. Sam beat her to the ice and was flying across the ice, her breath visible in the cold air. Jane edged onto the ice, biting her lip as she reminded herself to let her skates glide across the frosty surface. The air whipped around her each time Sam flew past. As children, they both had ice skáting lessons. Jane quickly found it was just a hobby for her, whereas Sam progressed through her exams, learning to pirouette and jump across the ice. Jane strained to hear her sister shouting something across the pond. 'I can't hear you, what did you say? You know, what?'

'I know you are having an affair with my husband.'

The words sliced through the air as a rush of air took Sam past her sister. Jane's knees trembled as the words took her breath away. She opened her mouth to speak, but no words came out. Her sister took the corner at the other end of the pond, building momentum as she approached Jane again, this time with no words. As Sam got closer, Jane saw her sister's leg leave the ice. The steel blade of the ice skate gleamed in the moonlight as it made contact with her neck. Sam's leg moved in a perfect arc, slicing her sister's neck before landing gracefully and propelling herself away from her husband's mistress.

The Promise

A good parent always keeps their promises.

6.45 am

'I'll be home before you know it!' Sara pulled on her jacket, then grabbed her toast from the plate before picking up her bag and giving one last wistful look at the scene in the living room. Her daughter, Maisie, begged Sara not to go to work on Christmas Eve. Sara had finally managed to stem her daughter's tears with promises she would be home early. As she left, Maisie called out, 'You promise, Mummy?'

'Whatever it takes, Angel, whatever it takes.' Sara promised.

Pulling the car into one of the allocated parking spaces, she glanced at the time on the dashboard – just long enough to run across the car park to the supermarket. Strolling into the office, cakes in hand, she smiled at her colleagues, who pounced on the goods before she had a chance to put them down.

‘Nice boppers!’ Katie observed laughing at her colleague. ‘Wouldn’t be so bad, except they are clearly made for a child’s head.’

Sara reached her hand to her head, pulling Maisie’s boppers off.

‘Oh, don’t. I was looking forward to explaining those to anyone we see out and about.’

‘I forgot they were there. Maisie wanted me to wear them for our Christmas Eve breakfast. Gosh, can you imagine if I forgot and we went out for a pickup with them on my head? Christmas or not, there would be murder!’

‘How is my precious little angel?’ Katie asked.

‘She’s okay. She was a bit upset that we won’t be spending the day together. It’s become our little tradition, and this is the first year I’ve had to work. When I left, she was busy deciding which dolls would be invited to her tea party, so hopefully she won’t miss me too much! I promised I would be home on time though, so we have to make sure we are out of the door at dead on 3 pm.’

‘Aye-aye, Captain. Anything to keep that sweet little girl happy. Bit jammy of you managing to get out of working Christmas Eve until now, though.’

‘You know I’ve always done extra in the run up to make up for it. It just didn’t work out that way this year.’ Sarah protested.

With Christmas plans discussed and cakes reduced to crumbs, the phone rang with perfect timing, giving them their first body removal of the shift. Katie and Sara slipped on smart jackets then checked the back of the unmarked van to ensure the equipment was all in place. Katie had taken the call and announced the grizzly murder scene to her colleagues, leaving Sara speculating as to where her colleague was driving them. With less offices open during the festive period, they were covering a bigger area today, and Katie took them back over the Tamar Bridge into Plymouth.

Katie bumped the van along the private lane off Mannamead Road until they pulled into the care home car park. The private road had seen little TLC in recent years with residents unable to reach an agreement as to how to split the bill, and the council maintaining it was nothing to do with them. The mixture of large Victorian and Edwardian houses made the area an attractive and affluent place to live, though the economy meant many were being converted into businesses such as care homes and nurseries, and others split into flats. The care home was previously a drug and alcohol rehabilitation centre until the government decided addiction treatment was no longer a hot topic and diverted funds elsewhere. The pale-yellow building, now adapted for elderly residents provided a quiet place to live their final days or years.

Before they could knock, the door was pulled open by the manager who greeted them with a friendly grimace, pulling down the bolts to open both of the double doors wide enough to allow entry to the four-wheeled stretcher.

Katie and Sara followed the manager into the spacious hallway with a high ceiling and parquet flooring. The space was painted a cheery yellow to match the exterior, with a few large pot plants to give the large area a homely feel. The formal signage and fire procedures on the walls gave away that it wasn't a private residence. That and the smell of cabbage with an undertone of antiseptic. The building retained many of its original features, and they were led through a heavy doorway to the part of the building housing ground floor residents. Most of the offices were upstairs to enable patients with mobility issues to take the downstairs rooms. The grand staircase was fitted with a stairlift for those unable to be allocated ground floor accommodation. The manager led them into the room, where they stood beside the bed, lowering their heads and observing a moment of silence before she passed them a clipboard.

'Everything you need should be on the paperwork – no pacemaker, before you ask. If there is anything you need, I'll be in the reception office.'

Katie glanced over the paperwork whilst Sara clipped a hospital-style wristlet around the deceased frail arm. When Katie indicated she was ready, Sara pulled a pair of blue latex gloves from her pocket and began checking the body. They lined the stretcher up with the bed and unzipped the thick black cadaver bag, preparing to transfer the body. Having worked many shifts together, they completed the process like a well-oiled machine until they were ready to zip the bag closed. The previously vacant corridor was now lined with staff and residents, heads bowed. Katie and Sara kept their heads down, avoiding eye-contact as they pushed the body through to the reception area. They wheeled him through the double doors and loaded the stretcher into the back of the van. As Katie started the engine, Sara spotted a face at the window, watching them. She clicked her teeth at Katie, nodding towards the window.

'Don't worry, Dear, we haven't forgotten you; your turn will come.' Katie joked. Seeing Sara's face, she continued. 'What?! We all know there is only one way out of this place, and it's not going to be clad in Lycra going for a run.'

9 am

Back in the office, Sara began completing paperwork, adding the elderly man's name to the whiteboard and filling in the mortuary register while Katie began to prepare the body, putting his head on a block and removing his pyjamas, ready to be dressed in a clean gown. They worked together, in relative silence, preparing the man's body for cold storage. Sara soaked a piece of cotton wool in disinfectant and handed it to Katie to plug the man's mouth, and they slid him into the large stainless steel refrigeration unit.

'Oh, for God's sake, are we never going to be able to have a cup of tea in peace?' Katie lamented as the office phone rang. 'It's another one at the care home. We're going to have to go back there. Might as well just set up cold storage at the care home and process them on site at this rate! I don't think the others will be back yet and they clock off soon anyway, so we best get out and get on with it.'

As the two women arrived back at the care home, the door opened, and the manager once again saw them in.

This time, the body was upstairs; Katie and Sara collapsed the stretcher. The manager gave them a tight smile and apologised for the lack of lift. The old buildings were solidly built, and even if the buildings weren't protected by a listed status, installing a lift would be a difficult and costly measure. Katie went in first and turned with a gleeful grin.

'Oh no, what is it? Why could you possibly be grinning like that?' Sara followed Katie's gaze and saw why she was smirking.

'I told you her time would come.' The lady who had been watching them from the window lay in the bed before them.

'Shhhh,' Sara hissed, 'she'll come back to haunt us.' The clipboard told them she passed away in her sleep, assumed natural causes, and the process of checking the body was problem-free. They carefully held the corners of the sheet as they lowered the body into the body bag on the stretcher. Zipping the bag with a flourish, Katie began strapping it to the stretcher, ready to upend it so they could manoeuvre it down the stairs.

Sara scanned the room and turned back to see Katie standing behind the upright stretcher, her arms stretched out either side as she waggled them, saying in a ghostly voice, 'I'm going to haunt you.' Stifling giggles, Sara took a deep breath and arranged her face with a solemn expression before opening the door to begin the journey to the car. Both women fell silent as they looked up at the now empty window, seeing nothing but an empty space where the woman once stood.

Sara's phone interrupted their conversation on the way back. Her daughter's face flashed on the screen, and she swiped to answer. Maisie's face filled the screen, her chocolate-streaked cheeks pre-empted Maisie's declaration that they had been baking. Sara laughed and turned the screen so Katie could see. 'Do you promise you will be home on time, Mummy?'

'Of course I will, Darling.' Sara looked at the corner of the screen. Just three more hours, and I will be home with you, so you had better keep me some of that chocolate cake.'

'How do you know we made chocolate cake?'

'Mummy's know everything. I need to get back to work now, but I'll see you in a few hours.'

'Do you promise?'

'I promise.' Sara confirmed before ringing off and reminding Katie she promised she would be home by three.

12 noon

Taking the body in and starting the refrigeration process, the colleagues once again worked in tandem completing the job. Adding the woman's name to the whiteboard and mortuary register and preparing her body left their work complete, and Katie groaned as she finally sat with a cup of tea and ginger nut. Hearing the door to the garage open, she flicked the kettle on as her colleagues stepped into the staffroom.

'Kettle's on, lads, if you fancy a cuppa before you get yours on ice?'

'Perfect, thanks, Katie.' Mal beamed at her as they retreated to unload the body and put it in the cool room, ready for preparation. Before Katie finished making the drinks, the phone rang with another request for a removal.

'Dropping like flies today. Another one.' She looked at Sara, who frowned at the clock.

Knowing they all wanted to finish on time, Mal smiled at Sara. 'Why don't we head out and pick this one up, and you carry on with the old bird we just left in the cold room? Then we can all get the last one done when we get back and be on our way.'

'Just as long as no more come in before whoever is next on shift arrives. It's typical, the one day I wanted to get out of here on time. I promised Maisie.' Katie rubbed her friend's arm, why don't you go and get started, and I'll help get the van loaded again and make sure everything is locked up. Then we will have her in the fridge in no time. Don't worry, that little girl has all of us backing her Christmas Eve tradition. We will get you home on time!'

Sara's smile didn't quite reach her eyes as she glanced at the screensaver on her phone - a family photo of her with her husband and daughter in Disneyland during the summer. Making her way through to the cold room, she picked up the clipboard where Mal had left it and unzipped the bag, chattering to the woman's body as she began to write on the whiteboard. Sara often spoke with the dead as she worked. 'Not long now, and we will have you all cleaned up. Just need to pop your name on one more register, and I can get you stripped off and into a gown.' She glanced at the door, wondering where Katie was. A noise caused her to spin back around, she expected to see Katie behind her laughing. The room was empty except for her and the body. Sara frowned. 'Did you hear that? Of course you didn't, you're dead.' The sound came again, and Sara stopped moving, cocking her head. It was quickly followed by a groan. Sara's heart raced as she looked at the open body bag. *Oh no.* They had all heard stories of people being brought to mortuary's or put in the refrigerator unit and woken up, but they were more like urban legends that didn't actually happen to people you knew. *Not today.* Sara looked at the clock again. *Not today.* She edged closer to the body and peered into the bag. The woman's eye lids flickered. She knew from the paperwork that the woman had been collected from a hospice. *How could they have not noticed she wasn't dead?!* She stepped back, frowning, and rubbing her temples. Gently pushing the door open, she looked around for Katie and was greeted with silence. The body groaned again. Sara looked at the clock. *The paperwork.* It was Sara's turn to groan. The paperwork that went with bringing a body to the mortuary that was still alive would take hours. They would need to call the police, the managers, the hospice. Sara's breath caught in her throat. The almost imperceptible ticking of the clock pierced her thoughts. Sara pictured Maisie's face if she didn't make it home on time, and stepped toward the body. She pinched the woman's nose, her palm covering her mouth. The woman groaned once more, and then nothing. Sara kept hold of her nose until the door opened, announcing Katie's arrival.

'Oi oi, the cavalry has arrived.' Seeing Sara's face, she stopped. 'Oh no, what's happened? Are you okay?'

Sara stared at Katie. Her hand now tucked up in her sleeve, hanging by her side.

Katie stepped closer and looked at the woman. 'Ah, shame. It's always expected to have the older ones in here, but this woman looks too young to die.' Sara said nothing. 'Can't be much older than us. Think it was a hospice pick up though, so nothing anyone could have done.'

'No.' Sara agreed, her voice a whisper.

'Right, come on, let's get her in the fridge and make space for when the last one comes in, and we can get you home to your little girl!'

'What if she's still alive?' Sara whispered.

Katie laughed. 'Don't be daft. That doesn't happen in real life. Imagine how many people would have had to have missed it if she was.'

'It happens, though.'

'Yeh, but not to us! Check for a pulse if it makes you feel better.'

Sara stepped towards the body and placed her forefinger and middle finger on the woman's wrist, letting out a breath as she was unable to find one.

'See! I told you so!' Katie said, snapping on a pair of gloves and unceremoniously shoving a wad of cotton wool into the woman's mouth.

Sara stepped into the warm living room and was immediately engulfed in a hug by two surprisingly strong little arms. Dropping her bag, she scooped her daughter into her arms.

'I thought you'd be late. You're always late home from work.' Maisie said accusingly.

'I made you a promise, Angel, and nothing was going to make me break my promise.'

Mistletoe Kisses

Kissing under the mistletoe is supposed to be good luck, right?

Friday

The porch light illuminated two figures laughing as they embraced beneath the mistletoe before disappearing inside. The doorstep was plunged into darkness, an upstairs light quickly replacing its yellow glow. From their vantage point, Kelly and Shannon had a clear view of the couple locked in a passionate embrace. The view was fleeting as the woman pulled the curtains closed.

'What a dick! An absolute bastard! He was never good enough for you. And did you see the state of her? Cheap box dyed hair'. Kelly shuddered. 'Shan? Are you okay?'

Shannon blinked slowly, then looked at the window. 'I think we've seen enough'.

'Where to?' Kelly asked.

'McDonalds and back to yours?'

Kelly nodded and started the car. 'Bastard.'

'Bastard.' Shannon echoed.

Fifteen minutes later, Shannon ripped open the brown paper bags, spreading their greasy feast of fast food on the table. Kelly popped the cork on a bottle of Prosecco and emptied it into two large wine glasses.

'What are you gonna do?'

'I dunno. I guess I'll find a divorce lawyer and get the ball rolling. Yay for me being a divorce statistic.'

'It's not your fault. He's the asshole. Thank God you didn't have children with him! Are you going to confront him?'

'I don't know. I don't think so. Not yet. I need time to think.'

'Okay, well, whenever you are ready to cut his clothes up, put hair remover cream in his shampoo or laxatives in his protein shake, let me know.'

Shannon laughed. 'I need to think about things before I do anything. I know I've suspected him for a while, but I guess a part of me just hoped I was wrong, hoped there would be an explanation.'

'I know, babe. You know I'm here for you. Whatever you need.'

Blinking back tears, she changed the subject.

Saturday

Opening one eye and then the other, Shannon groaned. She scanned the room, wincing as her eyes reached the ray of light peeping through the chink in the curtains. She kicked the duvet off and rolled onto her back, staring up at Kelly's living room ceiling until the churn of her stomach caused her to leap from the sofa. She made it to the kitchen, emptying her stomach into the sink. When there was nothing left to bring up, she ran the hot tap until all evidence of her stomach contents had been washed away. After rifling through the cupboards, Shannon retreated to the sofa armed with supplies: paracetamol, water, crisps. A ping alerted her to a text message from her husband: *Morning Gorgeous, how was your evening? Did you have a nice relaxing night to yourself? X.* Shannon sighed, the memories of the night before flashing through her brain like a show-reel. She squeezed her eyes shut and dropped her phone beside the sofa, fighting the pain of the knife stabbing her heart and the hangover gripping her head. Silent tears rolled down her cheeks. Another ping: *Everything okay? X.* Shannon sighed at her husband's follow up text and tapped a brief reply: *A bit fragile, had a few drinks with Kelly. Have a great day on the golf course today.* 'Golfing weekend, my ass,' Shannon muttered. She looked at her message, her fingers hovering over the keyboard before she added, *Love you x,* and hit send. 'Dickhead.'

'Squidge up, we having a pizza and duvet day or facing the world?' Kelly pulled the duvet over both their knees, scattering crumbs as she grabbed a handful of crisps and shoved them into her mouth.

'Could you fit any more in?!'

Kelly's jaw moved quickly as she crunched and opened her mouth, showing its contents to her friend.

'Minger.'

'You love me.'

'I feel like we should go out, but also, I would rather hide from the world. The longer we stay in this bubble, the longer I don't have to face up to things.'

A few hours later, the coffee table was littered with half-eaten pizzas and sides and credits rolled up the screen as Jude Law and Cameron Diaz got their festive happy ever after. Shannon turned to her friend. 'Okay, I'm ready. Tell me what my options are.'

Kelly reached for her iPad and began scrolling. 'Good news and bad news. You CAN divorce his cheating ass and blame his adultery, but he still might get his half of everything. Also, it looks like however you go about it, it's not a quick process.'

Shannon grabbed the iPad and swiped her finger up the screen, scanning the information. 'Fuck. Why does it all take so long? And why the fuck do I not get to take everything and fuck him over the way he has me?'

'It sounds like you are still in the anger stage of grief, and I am here for it. Let it all out.'

Shannon didn't reply as she continued scrolling.

Sunday

Shannon held a lighter to the wick of the pillar candle in the middle of the dining table, almost immediately pulling it back and blowing out the burgeoning flame. Putting the candle back in the drawer, she slammed it closed and sat at the table, drumming her fingernails. The clock ticked like a metronome in the quiet room until it was joined by the vibration of her phone. Shannon read the message from her husband: *Sorry, running late. Keep dinner warm for me. Looking forward to dessert ;).* 'Dessert,' Shannon scoffed, 'good luck with that, you cheating bastard.' The pot on the hob began to bubble, the metal saucepan lid emitting a tinny vibration as it wobbled on the pan. Shannon scanned the kitchen, an idea starting to form. She tapped a reply to her husband's message: *Don't worry, how about we skip dinner and I run us a nice bath instead? Love you. X.* She received a series of emojis in response. Removing the wine from the fridge, she poured a large glass, gulping it down before pouring the rest down the sink and dropping the bottle into the recycling.

Bubbles topped the steaming water, and Shannon smiled as she looked around the room, breathing in the musky aroma. A slam of the door signalled her husband's return. Butterflies flapped in her stomach, reminding her it would soon be over. As he reached the top of the stairs, Shannon turned to greet her husband with a kiss. 'How was your weekend?'

'Standard golf weekend, I won't bore you with the details.'

Shannon said nothing as she watched him strip and ease his body into the bath. She couldn't help but search it for signs of the other woman. He watched her eyes scan his body and reached her hand out pulling her close for a lingering kiss. Shannon squeezed her eyes closed, pushing the sickness down in her stomach. 'There is plenty of time for that. I realised we've run out of wine. I'll bring you up a snack while I run out and grab another bottle.'

Shannon took a deep breath and carried the tray up to the bathroom, careful not to trip on the extension lead. 'I've brought you up a bath picnic – toast and pate.' Shannon lay the tray on the stool beside the bath and smiled at her husband before picking up the toaster. She held it over the warm water.

'Hey, be careful with that! You want a husband to come home to!'

Shannon looked at him. The image of him kissing the woman on the doorstep flashed before her eyes and she let go of the toaster, jumping back, away from the sparks. The lights fizzed and went out, the room now dimly lit by the hallway lamp. As her husband's body thrashed, she stepped out, careful to avoid the water already spreading on the bathroom floor. Shannon watched from the door as his body stopped moving, his lifeless eyes staring at her. 'Divorce is so messy.' she declared as she put an end to her marriage.

The Snow Globes

Snow globes are one of the few places happiness is immortalised.

The winter sun dances around the room, bouncing between the watery globes. Dust shines in the air like snow suspended from falling. Every surface is filled with snow globes depicting festive scenes, each one a variation of the one before. Nothing bad happens in snow globes - I just know happy families are gathered inside the tiny cottages; I can almost smell the smoke coming from the chimneys on the snow-covered thatched roofs. Rainbows dance behind the dust particles where the light reflects around the room. The overall effect is magical.

'Don't leave them by the window,' Grandma used to say, 'the sun will start a fire.' Grandma was the only person who really got me. It's why she left me this house, not that there are any other choices now. Mum and Dad are long gone, and with Janine emigrating to New Zealand, it's been just me and Grandma for years. I've never even met my nieces.

I can't bring myself to change a thing in the house. Grandma died two years ago, and her dressing gown still hangs on the back of the bathroom door. I'm surprised the moths haven't come for it - I can't bring myself to wash it. I know it's silly, but I am sure it still smells of her. Her lavender talc and perfume are in the bathroom cupboard. Sometimes, I sprinkle talc on the bathmat, as if she was just there, as if she is in the other room getting dressed. If I close my eyes, I can hear her shouting for me to put the kettle on.

The snow globes were hers at first. She used to collect them. As kids, we would get her a new one every Christmas. After she died, I carried on the tradition; only, now, it's not just at Christmas. I search eBay and online shops for collectible globes. Janine used to send a globe from New Zealand every year, but now we are lucky if we even get a card. The sun shining in the window keeps the room warm, completely at odds with the snowy scenes, and sometimes I sit there for hours imagining the story within each little bubble. I once read that people attracted to snow globes are drawn to the childish pleasures of happy scenes and playing in the snow; a time of innocence before life got its mucky hands on us. That seems cynical, and makes the joy of them jaded somehow. Surely some people are just children at heart? The smell of dust particles burning reminds me of grandmas warning about them catching on fire.

I don't really leave the house anymore. It's too much for me, and there isn't any reason to go out when you can get everything delivered to your door. It's not just snow globes I collect. I also started collecting Christmas ornaments to make a model village. I have hundreds of them. I started on the dining table, creating the perfect winter wonderland. There are even little figurines that I can move around the village. I've always loved Christmas. When I was a little girl, Christmas was magical. Janine and I wore matching sweaters, put plates of food out for Father Christmas, and the whole family would eat together. Yes, Christmas was always a happy time.

I can't deny the house is getting a little cluttered now; perhaps collecting something smaller – maybe stamps or coins would have been more practical. Grandma's parcels and post still keep coming - her medication, her meals-on-wheels - though I do enjoy those. I haven't found a use for the incontinence pads - they are piling up. She used to have private carers, but after I kept turning them away, they eventually stopped coming. It didn't take long - you soon work out who is in the job for the money and who genuinely cares. I suppose they were useful for a while, but eventually, I thought it would be better just me and Grandma, so I just looked after her myself.

When she first died, I didn't think I could go on. It was just the two of us for so long; I couldn't envisage life without her and what that meant. It wasn't just life without her, it was the thought of a life alone. I remember looking at her medication and wishing I could join her. She took enough medication; it would have been easy to wash a few handfuls of pills down. I could have just drifted off in my sleep. Of course, I didn't. I found another way for us to stay together.

After she died, there was a smell at first. It hung around for months, lingering in the fabric of the rooms. I tried to air it. I ordered so many odour neutralisers. They all promised to banish bad smells. In the end, it just took time. And now? Now, she doesn't smell at all. I did have to change the bedding; she made quite a mess when she first died. Her skin has changed over the years, but we all change. Grandma's bone structure was always dainty, classically feminine, and as her skin shrank back against her bones, it only emphasised her beauty. These days, her skin is dark and waxy, but her hair is still the same. For a while, during those early days, we were both lost. But now, it's just like old times - the outside is another world. In here, it's just me and Grandma, remembering days gone by.

Shank

A prison drama, it's a bit sweary.

A large blob of phlegm landed on the desk in front of the Governor before Stephen felt his arms being pulled roughly behind him. He ignored the searing pain in his shoulders, smiling as he was led away, hands now cuffed in front of him.

'Don't let this be an excuse to start dicking around.' The officer said before Stephen was pushed into his cell. Most prisoners were at work or in education and the cell door slamming echoed on the quiet landing. Stephen looked around his cell, nostrils flaring. Turning, he slammed his palms on the door before punching it until his knuckles bled and there were smears of blood on the undamaged door. He ran his hands under the tap and sat on the hard bed, feeling the inflexible base through the thin mattress. His jaw clenched; his veins twitched. Steven sat there until prison movement began and the slamming of gates and jovial banter shattered the silence. Inmates were returning from their workplaces to eat lunch on the wing.

Heavy footsteps and the jangle of keys indicated an officer was on the landing; they stopped outside Stephen's door, and the privacy flap was opened.

'You're supposed to knock before opening that, what if I was having a shit.' Stephen challenged before the officer spoke.

'Well, you aren't, so it all worked out okay, didn't it.' The officer retorted. 'Do you want to come out for lunch or not?' He eyed Stephen's hands warily.

'It's alright, boss. I'll behave.'

The officer unlocked the door and stepped back. 'Don't let all the hard work go to waste. You can try for parole again in a few years.' Stephen clenched his jaw and said nothing. 'Do you want me to send a listener or a chaplain down?

'Are you joking?' Stephen spoke in a low voice. 'Are you fucking joking?'

'The offer is there if you want it. Now, why don't you calm down and go get some lunch.'

'Calm down?! Are you fucking having a laugh? I just had my freedom ripped from me. I'm not gunna get to go home to my missus and kids for Christmas, and you stand there telling me to calm down. All I do is jump through the hoops you pricks ask me to, and when it comes to getting something back, I get fuck all.'

The officer moved one hand to his baton while the other rested on his radio. Stephen stepped towards him. The officer held his ground. As other inmates arrived on the wing, noticing something was afoot, they flocked to the end of the wing where Stephen and the officer faced each other.

The shouting began.

'Hit him.'
'Fucking screws.'
'Go on Ste.'
'We have rights.'

The officer pressed a button on his radio as he drew his baton. Within seconds, the shouting intensified as more officers arrived on scene, shouting for inmates to return to their cells. The crowd partly dispersed, but the inmates jeering continued. Stephen looked at the officer. 'What are you gonna do, OFFICER?' he said pointedly as he took another step towards him. The small crowd shouted, with more inmates returning to the wing and standing in their doorways, watching the scene before them.

Officers pushed through the crowd and Stephen watched as something was passed between two inmates in his peripheral vision. He stepped away from them, drawing the officers toward him, leering at them. 'Oh look, back up. Come on then, officers, show me what you've got!'

Stephen danced on his toes in a boxing stance as the officers approached. The alarm sounded, and inmates continued to jeer. Those in their cells, banged the pipes by way of joining in the commotion. Surreptitiously watching the crowd, Stephen saw one person slip away and into a cell behind the commotion. Stephen continued his dance with the officers until he felt a sharp pain across the back of his legs. For a split second, he wobbled before regaining his stance and spinning to aim a punch at the officer who had delivered the strike. He landed a solid blow to his temple as the crowd erupted. Stephen felt another strike as a baton struck his side before officers pinned him to the floor. His cheek was pushed to the cold concrete floor, the knee in his back rendering him unable to move. As Stephen looked down the landing, he saw the inmate he had been watching emerge from the cell and nod at him before passing the item to one of his peers. Stephen was pulled to standing as he conceded. 'Alright, alright, I was only having a laugh. You boys don't know how to take a joke. It's lunchtime, lighten up.'

As Stephen was dragged from the wing, he glanced into the cell he had been watching, smiling at a prone figure surrounded by a red stain.

Kiss Me Quick

This story whisks you away to Vegas for a wedding. Will everyone survive to say, 'I do?'

27th December

Zoe looked at the white chiffon top and the rhinestone-embellished denim shorts laid out on the bed with a pair of sparkly white cowboy boots – her wedding outfit. As she reached out to pack them, her engagement ring caught the light. The antique ring had belonged to Jon's grandmother and, by chance, featured a sapphire which was Zoe's birth stone. She smiled at the memory of the day he proposed. They went for a walk around the local reservoir; he waited until the woodland opened into a clearing. The blue sky gave the illusion of summer, but the crisp air didn't allow them to forget it was only March. Jon waited until Zoe looked out at the view before he dropped to one knee and held the ring up, waiting until she turned to ask the question. Of course, she said yes immediately. With a stroke of luck, the ring fit and the perfect Instagram-worthy selfie with her hand held up to the camera was taken.

Zoe uploaded the photo, captioning it, *I said YES!!!!!! #Ido #MisstoMrs #bridetobe*

Finishing her packing and taking a picture of her suitcase, Zoe uploaded a photo to Instagram adding the all-important tags for maximum likes *#weddingready #vegas #vegaswedding #vegasbaby #goingtothechapel.* Watching the number of likes go up as people clicked on the heart, she smiled and threw her phone on the bed, zipping up the case ready for Jon to load into the car.

27th December

Jon handed the Range Rover keys to the attendant at the airport parking and assisted his friend with unloading the luggage onto the waiting trolleys. Paul had married his wife, Lucie, the year before with Jon by his side as best man. Lucie linked arms with Zoe, and the women walked ahead, leaving the men with their bags.

Luggage checked, extra baggage fees paid and champagne on ice, Lucie held her glass in the air and proposed a toast. 'To Jon and Zoe.' The four clinked their glasses and settled into easy conversation as they waited for their flight. Thanks to Zoe mentioning their upcoming nuptials to the air hostess, they had all been upgraded to first class and enjoyed a flight with all the trappings of luxury. Lucie and Zoe huddled together with a map of the strip, whilst Jon and Paul put their headphones in, fiddling with their individual TV screens.

The wedding was booked for 30th December, so they had a few days to fill before the big day. They booked to stay at the iconic Circus Circus Hotel. After checking in, and snagging a room upgrade, again due to the wedding, the foursome left their rooms to explore the strip. The evening was just beginning, and the air fizzed with energy. The casino sported an eclectic mix of guests, some wearing sliders and vests with jeans, others dressed in tuxedos with women in cocktail dresses on their arms. The large gaudy Christmas trees placed throughout the hotel wouldn't look out of place year-round. The hotel had been bought out and refurbished a few years previously but retained the RV park. The two couples were unperturbed by the less than complimentary, comments about the diverse range of people the RV park attracted. The airport taxi had dropped them at the understated rear of the hotel, so as they exited the front entrance, Zoe couldn't help but gasp at the bright lights and 123-foot neon clown. Paul made a joke about how many people it would kill if it fell, earning him a good-natured punch to the shoulder from Lucie.

'Seriously though,' he continued, 'the sign aside, I wonder how many people die in freak accidents in Vegas. It's the city of excess. Anything goes. I bet that clown could tell some tales about what it's seen!'

Warming to the theme, Jon joined in. 'I did read a post on Facebook about it not too long ago. I'm sure there were a few people that fell or jumped from the top of the Stratosphere, some helicopter rides that suffered mechanical failures and a good few rampages by mad men armed with guns or knives.'

'Jon! We are here for our wedding. I don't want to hear about man men running around with knives.'

'Don't worry, Woman. I'll protect you.' Jon spoke with a gravelly tone and flexed his bicep causing Zoe to giggle and lean in for him to kiss her on the cheek. He knew better than to kiss her lips when they were covered with gloopy shimmer.

Opening the door to a yellow taxi cab, he waited while Zoe and Lucie took selfies of them all with the cab in the background. The driver wove through the traffic, taking them to the dancing fountains at the Bellagio. The strip was busy with revellers, shoppers and showgirls looking to make money; there were even a few Santas. Two women sporting large headdresses and not a great deal else stepped towards Paul and John.

'I can think of another way they could die in Vegas if they think they are getting near those girls.' Zoe muttered to Lucie as they stepped between the women and their prey. The showgirls moved away, looking for their next targets to charge for a photo and the hint of something that was never going to happen.

The music started, causing a surge of people to step closer to the fountains, keen to watch the famous jets swaying in time with the music. Zoe took her camera out, pouting as she took a selfie of her and Lucie. Jon rolled his eyes at Paul. After Zoe had finished uploading the photo to her social media - *#Bellagio #WhathappensinVegas #dancingfoundatins* - Jon took the opportunity to stand behind her, wrapping his arms around her chest and nuzzling into her neck.

'I love you, Mrs Webster.'

'I'm not Mrs Webster yet.'

'No, but you soon will be, and I can't wait. And then it won't be long before there are mini Websters.'

'Plenty of time for all that. Let's just enjoy each other and being a married couple before we rush into anything. We have all the time in the world.' Zoe kissed Jon on the lips, leaving a sticky residue. When she turned back to the fountain, he discreetly wiped his mouth with the back of his hand.

28th December

After a leisurely morning, Paul and Jon were instructed to entertain themselves whilst Zoe and Lucie went in search of the perfect Stetson to complete Zoe's wedding outfit. Tradition dictated Jon couldn't see Zoe's outfit before the wedding, and she didn't want to ruin one trying to hide it in a suitcase. Exiting the Uber outside the custom hat shop that Google suggested should be their first port of call, the women stopped for a moment to survey the tall man leaving the shop. He wore a checked shirt (or plaid, as they discovered the Americans called it), cowboy boots and a Stetson. Despite the festive season, his skin held a deep tan, and his jeans perfectly displayed his pert posterior.

'I wouldn't kick him out of bed.' Lucie declared.

'You're married. It's not too late for me. The wedding's off!' Zoe's eyes followed him as he strutted past them.

'Afternoon Ladies.' The cowboy acknowledged them with a deep southern drawl as he dipped his hat in their direction.

Their eyes followed him as he walked away, disappearing around a corner, where his horse was saddled and waiting to take him off into the desert, they speculated. The next customer leaving the shop broke their reverie. Another cliché in the city where anything could happen, and they giggled at the short, portly man who clearly thought dressing like an oil tycoon from a soft porn novel would make up for his otherwise unappealing stature. Not stopping to watch this one, they headed for the hat shop, immediately greeted by a unique smell. Zoe sniffed the air, inhaling the woody aroma. The shop didn't just sell hats and the walls were adorned with leather chaps, cowboy boots and fringed waistcoats to ensure every outfit was complete. Lucie fingered the suede fringe, letting the fronds fall between her fingers. 'Is it me, or is there a Fifty Shades vibe in here?'

'Ha. It's the cowboy getting us all worked up!' Zoe retorted, seeing the sign prohibiting photography and automatically scanning for cameras. Seeing none, she held her phone up, pouting for the camera and holding her fingers up in the peace symbol. *#weddingshopping #vegas #bridetobe #cowgirls*

'Well, now I know you saw the sign. I saw you looking for cameras after you read it. So, do you want to buy something, or are you just here to gawp? If it's the latter, I suggest you leave.' The busty woman held a large rifle by her side. Zoe's eyes widened as she backed away, reversing into Lucie, whose feet remained glued to the floor. The woman followed their eyes to the gun, and she threw her head back, letting out a hearty laugh. 'You should see your faces. This ain't loaded. I was just out the back cleaning some of our *more specialist* stock. Now, I assume you gals came here for something rather than to ignore my photography policy. What can I do you for?' The woman leaned the gun against the counter, her large breasts jiggling as she laughed.

'W- wedding.' Zoe stammered, her usual confidence MIA. Lucie stepped forward, taking charge and letting the woman know they were looking for the finishing touches for Zoe's wedding outfit.

'Well, why didn't you say. Come on through, I have a whole rack of bridal stuff in the back room, hats and chaps, boots and suits. I even have the odd leather whip if you are into that kind of thing.' She winked at them. Earlier awkwardness was quickly forgotten as the wedding became the focus. Choosing their items and arranging for the white feathered Stetson to be personalised for collection the following day, Lucie asked for directions to the Wedding Chapel. The woman frowned. 'Make sure you take a cab. It's getting dark, and you don't wanna be walking out there on your own at night.'

'I thought Vegas was safe enough - there are always lots of people around?' Lucie asked.

'Not after dark, not this side of the strip. You don't want to walk around on your own this side of the Stratosphere. We don't just sell guns; I keep one on me at all times, for protection.' Putting her hand down her top, she produced a small shiny handgun. 'And believe me, I've had to use it on more than one occasion.'

As she waved the gun around, Zoe's eye followed it. 'Is that thing loaded?'

'Yes.'

'Jesus! We were joking before about me becoming a widow before I even make it down the aisle, but I don't want to die either! Please, stop waving that thing around!' She kept her tone light but didn't take her eyes off the gun.

'Remember what I said?' The woman reminded them about staying safe before her tone reverted to the camaraderie they established previously. She thanked them for shopping there and reminded them to pick up their purchases after noon the next day.

Exiting the hat shop, flagged down a yellow cab that took them to the chapel. They had poured over the video tour on the website, imagining what the venue would look like. Mara, the wedding planner, greeted them – a sensible girl with flat shoes and straight hair. Her pale skin gave her a slight English Rose aesthetic; she wouldn't look out of place in England, but amongst the bright lights of Vegas, her normalcy was lost. Sighing, she explained her mother and step-father owned the business and she worked there whilst she saved to go back to school. Leading them through the gaudily tinsel-decorated foyer, she pushed open a set of double doors that led into a plain room with two neat rows of chairs. The white chairs were carved to match the ornate wood carving on the doors and furniture. The front of the chapel had a step up to a platform that held a plain arch.

'We're closed to weddings today, so the chapel is bare while everything is washed and polished, ready for the next ceremony, but we will have it looking like we discussed on the Zoom calls. We'll leave the Christmas decorations up in the foyer until after New Year.' She indicated cameras in the corner of the room. 'Your live stream link will have two camera angles, and the photographer will try to stay out of them when possible. Do you have any questions?'

'No, I just wanted to see the space beforehand. It's hard to get an idea of size from the pictures, but this all looks great! Zoe looked at the wall of photos in the foyer. 'Is Elvis here?'

Mara sighed and pursed her lips. 'No, he has another gig elsewhere today. We need to change those photos as a new Elvis just started.'

'Ah, I'm *all shook up*, I thought he would be here today to *kiss me quick*.' Zoe giggled, looking at Lucie, who rolled her eyes. The wedding planner didn't react. 'Oh, come on! Neither of you going to laugh with me?! What happened to the old Elvis, then? It sounds like there is a story there.'

'Or do you just have a *suspicious mind*.' Lucie chipped in, warming to the theme.

'No story, I'm afraid. We just want to make sure you have the best wedding experience. He was with us a long time, but it was time for him to move on.'

Mara wouldn't be drawn into further discussion and quickly moved them along, pointing to a waiting cab. 'Well, she was a barrel of laughs!' Zoe observed when they were safely in the cab to Fremont Street. The bright strobe lights and music flooded their senses as they exited the cab. Paying the driver, Zoe took a few photos, and they looked around until they spotted Jon and Paul. The men were both worse for wear, and Zoe and Lucie quickly purchased some fruity drinks in test tubes from a girl in a catsuit with a V-neck that plunged to reveal her belly button. They downed three each before declaring it looked like dinner would be liquid. The party atmosphere on Fremont Street pulled them into its clutches, keeping them drinking, dancing and partying until they passed out in their rooms, fully clothed.

29th December

Hearing the flush, Jon groaned and peeled his face from the pillow. He blinked until his eyes adjusted to the dim light and saw Zoe returning from the bathroom. She gave a smiling grimace before croaking that it had been a good night. Throwing a towel at her fiancé, she pulled on jeans and a hoody and slouched at the dressing table, staring at her pale face. Ten minutes later, both showered and dressed, they met Lucie and Paul at the elevator and left the hotel, instructing a waiting cab to take them to the Stratosphere. The breakfast buffet did not disappoint and the two couples travelled to the Observation Deck, hangovers alleviated. Zoe took photos of the desert view before they moved vantage points and took in the strip. Lucie exclaimed as she spotted the Circus Circus big top, followed quickly by other landmarks - the large flat structure of Treasure Island and the green MGM Grand.

'Anyone fancy going on the rides?' Paul asked, pointing at the fairground-style attractions suspending tourists over 1,000 feet above the strip.

'Rather you than me, but I'll happily take photos of your terrified faces if you do.' Zoe taunted.

'I need a lot of alcohol before you would get me out there,' Paul confessed, 'and even then, I'm not sure there is enough alcohol to convince me that that ride doesn't put me at a high risk of sudden death.'

Zoe quipped that she needed the ring on her finger first so she could get the life insurance payout. 'Anyway, death defying activities aside, who fancies a ride down the strip to the Las Vegas sign? I just want to pop by the hotel first, now I feel more alive, and make myself more presentable.'

'Sort out your hair and makeup so you can take better photos with the sign to get likes from your followers more like.' Seeing his fiancé's face, Jon reassured her he didn't mind. 'I knew about your online army of followers when I met you, and I love you *in spite* of them! And I have faith that one day you will achieve your dream of going viral.'

The Uber driver dropped them by the famous Las Vegas sign, and they joined the queue of tourists waiting to have their photo taken with it. 'I didn't expect a queue!' Lucie observed.

'I know, right?! Instagram vs reality.' Zoe replied. 'It was the same when we went to Lands End in Cornwall, though I don't think you can get a photo with the sign down there anymore.'

'You did *not* just compare Vegas with Cornwall!' Lucie chided her friend.

They waited in line until their turn and took a selection of photos, much to the chagrin of the people behind them. Zoe and Lucie pulled Santa hats from their bags and handed them to Jon and Ian so they could pose for a festive group photo. Jon tried in vain to chivvy Zoe and Lucie along, earning the response from Zoe, 'What are they gunna do? Shoot me?'

'Ha.' Jon replied. 'Although, statistically, the odds of being shot are probably significantly higher here, so let's get a move on before you hogging the sign makes me a widower. We can walk back up the strip and get some presents to take back. I need to get something for my nieces.'

Thinking of the gun they had waved in their faces the day before, Zoe shuddered and glared at her fiancé. 'You know, you shouldn't make jokes like that.'

'Come on, babe. You know it's only a joke. Nothing's actually going to happen.' Jon wrapped his arm around his future bride.

The group began the walk back up the strip. They ducked in and out of various shops and snack bars, and made the obligatory stop at the M&M shop. 'Hey, look!' As they exited the store, Lucie pointed to a billboard. 'It's our cowboy.' The 'cowboy' from the hat shop featured on a poster along with five other cowboys promoting the 'Wild West Striptease'.

'No. Absolutely not. We're not going to a strip show.' Paul answered before Zoe and Lucie could pose the question. 'Besides, we have a wedding tomorrow and I thought you girls were booked in at a spa this evening.'

Lucie gave an exaggerated huff and drifted toward the enormous individual pizza slices being sold on a cart by a street vendor.

30th December – The Wedding Day

Zoe sprang out of bed, then looked around at the unfamiliar surroundings. Lucie stirred in her sleep as Zoe opened the curtains in Lucie and Paul's room. They were meeting the men at the chapel. Lucie groaned, pulling the cover over her head. Zoe bounded to the bathroom belting out the Dixie Cups, Going to the Chapel of Love, destroying all chances of Lucie going back to sleep.

Zoe emerged from the bathroom amidst a cloud of steam. She sat on the bed and scrolled through the messages on her phone. The UK was eight hours ahead, so she had been receiving wedding day well wishes for many hours while she slept. She snapped a photo of her cowboy boots and uploaded it to her social media, *#weddingday #soontobemrs #vegaswedding #chapeloflove #elviswedding.* She took a moment to watch the likes and comments on her post, smiling at the screen before moving to the dressing table to begin her hair and makeup.

The midday wedding meant their friends, family and Zoe's social media followers in the UK could watch it without staying up too late. Pulling up at the chapel, the wedding coordinator spoke into an earpiece, and Elvis appeared, holding the door open for them to enter the chapel.

'Jon and um,' the wedding coordinator looked down at her clipboard, 'Paul, are inside. Elvis will walk you up the aisle, as we discussed, and will then take his place to perform the ceremony. Do you have any last questions?'

Zoe shook her head, checking her Stetson was in place before taking a deep breath and holding her arm out to Elvis. Mara opened the door to the chapel, and music started as Elvis and Zoe walked up the aisle. Jon's gaze fixed first on her boots, then trailed up her legs to her hot pants. 'I love that you still perve on me, but my face is up here!' Zoe laughed and directed her fiancé's chin to her face for a kiss.

'Hey there! Isn't there supposed to be a wedding before any of that?!' Elvis took control of the ceremony, and the music dimmed as he began the service by waving at the camera and greeting those watching via live stream. 'Now, first of all, I have to ask if anyone here knows of any reason why these two stunning individuals should not be joined in holy matrimony today?' The photographer, wedding coordinator, Paul and Lucie remained silent, and he continued with the vows until the time came for him to drawl the words 'ah now pronounce you man and wife. *Now*, you may kiss the bride.' Zoe wrapped her arms around Jon's neck and pulled him close for a long kiss to cheers and whoops from Paul and Lucie. Elvis directed them all to turn towards the camera to wave and give any messages before the photographer would take some posed photos. As the group smiled into the camera, their cheery messages were interrupted by a banging. Glancing at Elvis, the wedding planner apologised and hurried from the room. Moments later, the crack of gunshot preceded the door to the chapel swinging open.

Zoe, Jon, Paul and Lucie all looked at the Elvis standing in the doorway. His white jumpsuit, adorned with rhinestones, matched their Elvis. The only difference was, whilst their Elvis held a microphone, the new one held a handgun.

'What are you playing at, Jeff?' The southern drawl was now gone, and Elvis spoke with a harsh New York accent.

'You! You took my job. You took my job, and now I hear you also came after my missus.'

Elvis stared at Jeff, his mouth opening and closing. The other wedding attendees stood frozen in their positions; the red light on the camera continued to blink.

'There's nothing left for me anymore. You took it all. And now you have to pay.'

Zoe's phone vibrated in her bra, and she glanced at the camera before looking at her new husband, and then at the gun. She gulped, stepping closer to Paul. At her movement, Jeff raised the gun. 'Where do you think you're going?' Zoe stammered an apology and stepped away from her new husband.

'Come on, man, let the tourists go. This is between us. This is our battle, nothing to do with them.' Elvis pled with Jeff, holding his hands up as he made eye contact.

'Yeh. I didn't sleep with anyone's wife.' Paul said.

Jeff turned to Paul and shattered his kneecap with one click of the Glock. Screaming, Lucie dropped to her knees beside her husband's writhing body. Her hands quickly became covered in blood as she tried to stem the blood pouring from the wound just above his knee.

'Oh, for God's sake. Be quiet, or I'll put a bullet in both of you.' He turned his attention to Zoe who was looking into the camera, her lips moving as she tried to tell her mother she loved her. 'What the fuck are you doing? Did I tell you to move?'

Zoe shook her head.

'Jeff, buddy.' Jon took the attention from his new Bride.

'Buddy?! Do I look like your buddy?' Jeff inched closer to the group. 'He was supposed to be my buddy.' He waved the gun in the direction of Elvis. 'He was supposed to be my buddy, but not anymore. He told my boss I'm a drunk so he could take my job, then he slept with my wife. So, I don't need any more buddies. Actually, I've had enough of you. Get over there on the floor with your *buddy.*' He nodded towards Paul. Jon stepped closer to Zoe.

'Oh. Come. On. She will only cheat on you. That's what they all do. I'll tell you what, I'll do you a favour.' In one swift movement, Jeff aimed the gun towards Zoe and pulled the trigger.

Zoe stumbled backwards, dropping her phone as her hands flew to her chest. She tried to speak, but the words wouldn't come out. Lucie's screaming caused her to look around; her friend's face was etched with terror. In what felt like slow motion, she turned her head to her husband. He was always calm. He would know what to do. She looked at her chest, thinking she would never get the blood out of her white top. As she tried to breathe in, the air bubble in her chest caused a gurgle. Zoe's eyes were wide with panic as she tried to focus on the room. They came to rest on her mobile phone and she smiled faintly as the likes and notifications lit up the screen, her final thought that she finally went viral.

...and they all lived happily ever after.

The End

Acknowledgements

They say it takes a village; well this book baby really did! I have sent various versions of short stories to so many friends and family for feedback and support along the way, I can't possibly name you all – that makes me sound terribly popular, doesn't it? It's just a cover for what a hermit I really am!

As always, here through thick and thin – Tracey. Thanks go to my lovely editor who puts up with my aversion to commas, apostrophes, and well, properly editing my own work because I prefer to leave it to her! (Tracey ann-Plater if you need an editor!)

Write Magic – the fabulous gang of writers, always there to motivate and support, some of whom I have the pleasure of calling friends beyond the writing group.

Kadie – the final murders we giggled over are in this one. So, for the last time, thank you x

Until next time,

Caroline xx

Also by C.M. Serpell…

UNTIL DEATH

'Until death us do part.'

He meant it.

'All Catherine wanted was a happy ever after.
Swept off her feet by a charming lawyer, she learned not all fairy tales have a happy ending.

Sometimes death is the only escape.

Someone knows what you did...
Revenge is coming.'

Also by C.M. Serpell…

HER

If one of the good guys is killing the bad guys, is she a hero or a villain?

She works for the local authorities and is on a killing spree in Plymouth. She only kids bad guys. That makes it okay, right?

She said she will help you get your life back on track.
She told you, you are worth more than this.
She said she wants to help.
It's her job.

She said you should have done more.
She told you, you had your chance to change
She said she can't stand by and watch you destroy others.
It's you next.

Printed in Great Britain
by Amazon

50894797R00061